Princess Truly

Off I Go!

WRITTEN BY
**Kelly
Greenawalt**

ART BY
**Amariah
Rauscher**

❡ACORN™
SCHOLASTIC INC.

To Christin McQueen, world traveler. Your confidence and free spirit are TRULY inspiring. And to Chuck Greenawalt, amazing husband. Home is wherever you are. — KG

To my family, my favorite people to go with on adventures. — AR

Text copyright © 2019 by Kelly Greenawalt
Illustrations copyright © 2019 by Amariah Rauscher

Library of Congress Cataloging-in-Publication Data

Names: Greenawalt, Kelly, author. | Rauscher, Amariah, illustrator.
Title: Off I Go! / by Kelly Greenawalt ; illustrated by Amariah Rauscher.
Description: First edition. | New York, NY : Acorn/Scholastic Inc., [2019] | Series: Princess Truly | Summary: Told in rhyming text, Princess Truly uses her super powers to explore the world, whether it is visiting penguins with her brother in Antarctica, or taking her timid pug Sir Noodles on a vacation in a rain forest.
Identifiers: LCCN 2018053886| ISBN 9781338340037 (pbk.) | ISBN 9781338340068 (hardcover)
Subjects: LCSH: Princesses—Juvenile fiction. | Superheroes—Juvenile fiction. | Explorers—Juvenile fiction. | Brothers and sisters—Juvenile fiction. | Pug—Juvenile fiction. | Stories in rhyme. | CYAC: Stories in rhyme. | Princesses—Fiction. | Superheroes—Fiction. | Explorers—Fiction. | Adventure and adventurers—Fiction. | Brothers and sisters—Fiction. | LCGFT: Stories in rhyme.
Classification: LCC PZ8.3.G7495 Gr 2019 | DDC [E]—dc23 LC record available at https://lccn.loc.gov/2018053886

10 9 8 7 6 5 4 3 2 1   19 20 21 22 23

Printed in China   62

First edition, December 2019

Edited by Rachel Matson
Book design by Sarah Dvojack

Up and Away We Go

I am Princess Truly.
I love to explore.

I go to new places

I have not seen before.

I live for adventure.
There is so much to see!

4

The world is amazing.
Come fly along with me.

We will meet fun new friends.
We can go anywhere.

The sky is the limit,
with magic curly hair.

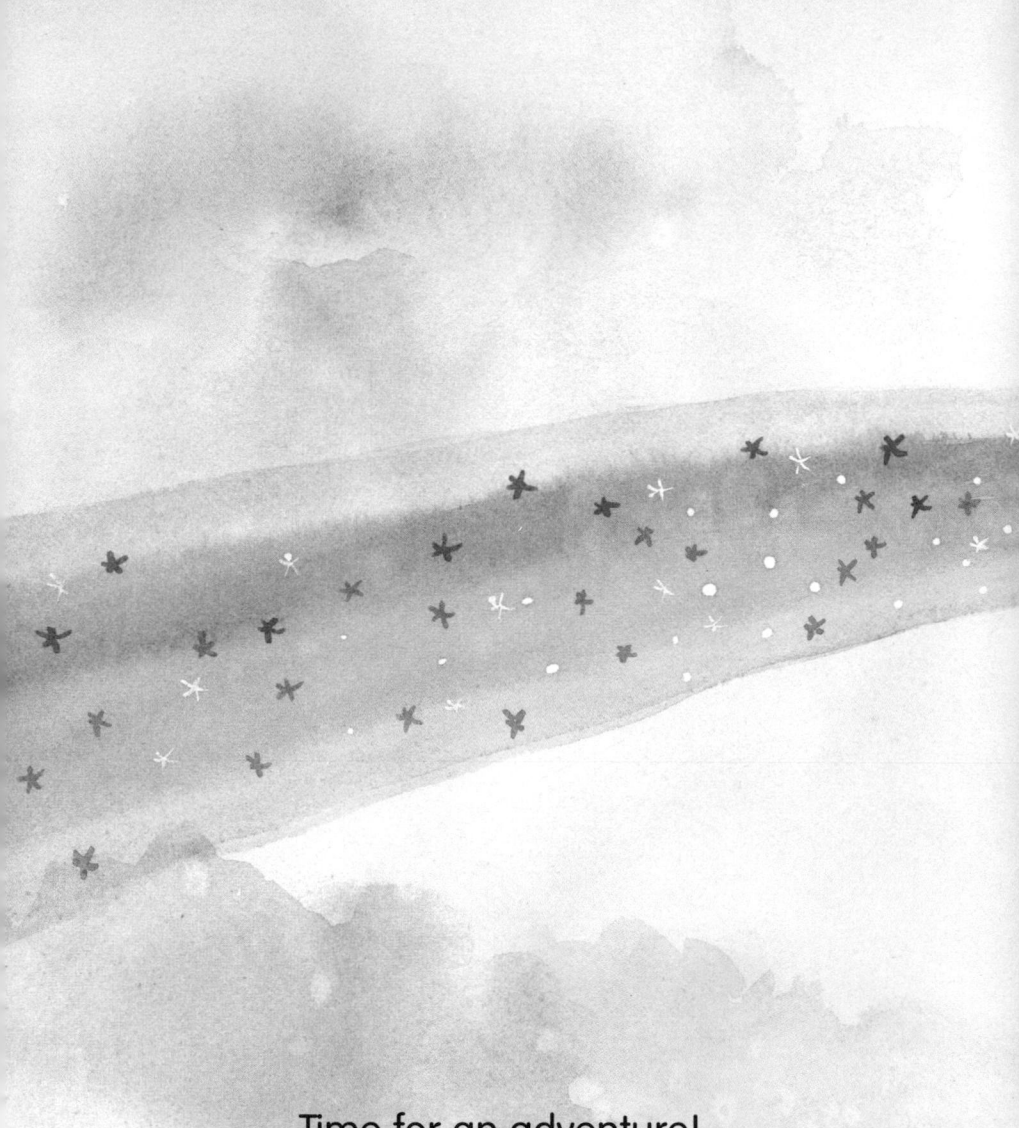

Time for an adventure!
My curls begin to glow.

We are brave explorers.
Up and away we go!

Penguins at the Pole

Let's go to the South Pole!
I want to see the snow.

My brother loves penguins.
Ty really wants to go.

We fly over the ice,

then see a pod of whales.

They are very friendly.
They wave "hi" with their tails.

Next, we see tall penguins.
They waddle on the ice.

14

I see they have webbed feet.

Their flippers are so nice!

It is time for dinner.
The penguins need to fish.

We want to go with them.
I make a magic wish.

My curls start to sparkle.
They twinkle and they glow.

Hooray! We have flippers.
Now all of us can go.

One penguin will not move.
She looks like she might cry.

She is afraid of heights.
The ice is just too high.

I give her an umbrella,
and tell her she can glide.

She floats down to the sea.
We all zoom by her side.

We explore the ocean.
We dive down very deep.

24

The penuins eat their fish.
But then they want to sleep.

25

The South Pole has been fun,
but now we say good-bye.

26

Off to a new adventure,
with Noodles and with Ty!

Home Sweet Home

Sir Noodles is my dog.
He's been a grumpy pup.

I planned a trip for us.
That will cheer him right up!

We hop on a pink boat,
to find the perfect spot.

We go to an island,
but Noodles is too hot.

The beach is too crowded.
He does not like the sand.

32

He does not want to swim.

He just wants to be fanned.

So we get on a jet.
We go to the city.

34

I like seeing the lights.
They shimmer so pretty.

Noodles does not think so.
He thinks they are too bright.

The car horns are too loud.
He cannot sleep at night.

To the rain forest next!
We take a speedy flight.

He does not like the bugs.
He thinks that they might bite.

The tiger looks scary.

And the frog makes him run.

He sees a curly snake!

He isn't having fun.

So off we go again!

Sir Noodles wants some rest.

I love our adventures,
but he likes home the best.

About the Creators

Kelly Greenawalt is the mother to six amazing kids. She lives in Texas with her family. Her favorite place to visit is the snowy mountains of Colorado. Princess Truly was inspired by her oldest daughters, Calista and Kaia, who love to go on adventures.

Amariah Rauscher is the mom of two girls who both love to explore new places. Her favorite places to visit are Japan and New Orleans. But just like Sir Noodles, she likes home the best, where she spends many hours painting, drawing, and reading books.

Read these picture books featuring Princess Truly!

YOU CAN DRAW NOODLES!

1. Draw an outline of Noodles's body. Add his back foot.

2. Add his two front feet. Add ears.

3. Draw his eyes and triangle nose.

4. Draw an upside-down "m" for the mouth.

5. Add his tongue and...

6. Color in your drawing!

WHAT'S YOUR STORY?

Princess Truly is an explorer.
Where would **you** like to go?
How would you get there?
Who would you meet?
Write and draw your story!